Amy Loves the Sun

by Julia Hoban

pictures by Lillian Hoban

Harper & Row, Publishers

Amy Loves the Sun
Text copyright © 1988 by Julia Hoban
Illustrations copyright © 1988 by Lillian Hoban
Printed in Singapore

Library of Congress Cataloging-in-Publication Data
Hoban, Julia.
    Amy loves the sun.

    Summary: Amy picks some flowers on a sunny day and
gives them to her mother.
    [1. Flowers—Fiction.   2. Mother and child—Fiction]
I. Hoban, Lillian, ill.   II. Title.
PZ7.H63487A1 1988   [E]   87-45987
ISBN 0-06-022396-0
ISBN 0-06-022397-9 (lib. bdg.)

                1 2 3 4 5 6 7 8 9 10
                First Edition

Amy Loves the Sun

It is a sunny day.

Amy runs through the grass.

The sun shines on the grass
and makes it warm.

The warm grass is soft on
Amy's bare toes.

The sun shines on the flowers.
Yellow dandelions, white daisies.

The daisies have yellow centers.

Amy picks four dandelions
and one daisy.

There is a bumblebee.
He is smelling the flowers.

Amy smells the flowers too.

The flowers smell like sunshine.

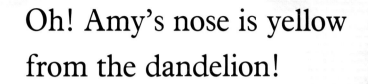

Oh! Amy's nose is yellow
from the dandelion!

There is a caterpillar on the daisy.

It is soft and fuzzy.
Its fuzz feels so warm in the sun.

Amy gives Mommy
the flowers.

Thank you, Amy.

Mommy will put
the dandelions in water.

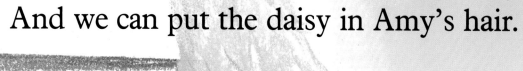

And we can put the daisy in Amy's hair.